Tilly
AND THE
Badgers

For Shona, Amy, Rosa and Aedan.
J.L.

Also by Joan Lingard
Tilly and the Wild Goats

ORCHARD BOOKS
338 Euston Road, London NW1 3BH
Orchard Books Australia
Hachette Children's Books
Level 17/207 Kent St, Sydney, NSW 2000
ISBN 978 1 84616 287 9 (paperback)

First published in Great Britain in 2006
A paperback original

A CIP catalogue record for this book is available
from the British Library.

1 3 5 7 9 10 8 6 4 2 (hardback)
5 7 9 10 8 6 4 (paperback)

Printed in Great Britain by Cox & Wyman, CPI Group.

Tilly
AND THE
Badgers

JOAN LINGARD

Illustrated by Ann Kronheimer

ORCHARD BOOKS

CHAPTER 1

"Isn't it terrible," said Tilly's mum, "that people could do such a thing?"

"What thing?" asked Tilly, squinting to see what her mother was reading in the local paper, the *Gazette*.

"Bait badgers?"

"How do you mean – *bait* them?"

"Set dogs on them, to fight them. For sport."

"*For sport?*" echoed Tilly.

"Here, see for yourself." Her

mother passed over the paper.

Tilly read the headline.

She looked up from the paper. "Why don't the police stop them?"

"They usually can't catch them in the act. The trouble is the police have more than enough to do. Catching thieves and so forth."

They knew all about catching thieves. Mr Sheridan, who lived in the big house, had had his silver stolen by two people who'd been working for him and whom he'd trusted. It was Tilly and her friend William who had found them out.

Tilly and her mother lived in the gate lodge at the foot of Mr Sheridan's drive. They loved the neat little stone house with rambling roses growing round the front door. Tilly thought it looked like a house out of a fairy tale .

"You'd better get a move on, Tilly." Her mum looked at the clock. "At this rate, you're going to be late for school!"

"Can I take the paper with me? I want to read about the badgers." They always started school with news of the day.

"OK, but bring it back. I haven't finished it yet."

Tilly folded the paper and put it in her backpack.

"Have you brushed your hair? I thought not! You can't go out like that."

Tilly seized the brush and gave her marmalade-coloured hair a few quick strokes. It was a bit tangly. "That'll have to do."

"And don't forget your lunch box!" Her mum shook her head. "Honestly, I think you'd forget your head if it wasn't tied on."

Tilly squashed the box into her bag, which was now so full that she could just fasten the straps and no more. Then she set off along the road, watched by her mum, who always stood at the bottom of the drive until she reached the cottages at the edge of the village. When Tilly got there she would turn and wave and her mum would go back inside.

William lived at number 3 Bank Cottages. He was waiting at his gate.

"You're late," he grumbled. He was never late.

"Only a minute or two. I was reading about badgers."

"Badgers?"

"You know, those furry animals that come out at night." She was teasing him. Of course he knew what badgers were! She danced out of his reach. They had once found one lying dead in the road. They had decided it must have been knocked down by a car during the night.

"So what about them?" asked William.

"People bait them."

They could hear the school bell ringing. They began to run.

"I told you you were late," puffed William.

"Come on then, you two!" cried Mr Flynn, the janitor, who was standing at the school gate. "Cutting it fine, aren't you?"

They had arrived in time to tag on to the end of the line. It was not a big line, since they only had twenty-four children in the school altogether, from primary one to seven, and two teachers.

Tilly and William were in the upper part of the school. They were sitting in their classroom when their teacher, Mrs Graham, came in with a new boy. Everyone was immediately interested, for it was not often that they had a new pupil in school. They couldn't help noticing that everything about him looked brand new, his jeans, his sweatshirt, his trainers. The trainers were an expensive make.

"This is Cecil," Mrs Graham announced, giving him a warm smile. She had a nice smile though she could frown, too, on occasion. "I want you all to welcome him into our class."

"Cecil," sniggered Billy Black behind his hand. He sniggered at the slightest thing so the rest of the class paid no attention, except for the new boy. His eyes flickered for a moment then his face went still again. Almost blank, you might say.

Mrs Graham frowned and eyed Billy sternly but she said nothing. She put Cecil into a desk next to William and asked William to look after him.

Cecil didn't even give William a glance as he sat down.

It was news time. Mrs Graham asked if anyone would like to begin and Tilly's hand shot up straightaway. It often did. She took out the *Gazette*, unfolded it and began to read.

"It has come to light that the barbaric practice of badger-baiting is still going on in Scotland."

"What does barbaric mean?" Mrs Graham asked the class.

"Uncivilised," said the new boy without bothering to put his hand up first. But then he wouldn't know how they did things. He had said it in a bored kind of way, as if any idiot should know the answer.

"Very good, Cecil," said Mrs Graham. "Carry on, Tilly."

Tilly read carefully, taking her time. "This ancient and illegal sport consists of badgers being forced to fight to the death with dogs, usually terriers. Sometimes terriers crossed

14

with pit-bull terriers are used." She paused, then continued. "The badgers are put in the middle of a ring and the dogs are set on them."

"Yuck," said Kirsty Flynn, the janitor's daughter.

"It certainly is a very cruel sport." Mrs Graham gave a little shudder.

Everyone was in agreement about that though Cecil, Tilly saw, said nothing.

"Where would they get the badgers from?" asked Angus Robertson.

"From their setts, of course," said Cecil.

"But they're not easy to find," Angus retaliated.

"Those people obviously know how to," rejoined Cecil. "Or they wouldn't be able to bait the badgers, would they?"

"Carry on, Tilly," said Mrs Graham.

"They take the badgers to a secret, remote place. That's what makes it so difficult for the police. Sometimes as many as forty people come to watch the fight."

"Forty?" repeated Kirsty Flynn. "You'd think somebody would see them and tell on them."

"Seems they don't," said Tilly. "They put bets on who'll win. The dog or the badger."

"That means both the dogs and the badgers must end up injured," put in William.

"I'd have thought the badgers would be stronger," said Matthew Mackie.

Tilly was still reading. "You're right! If they are, they break their jaws or legs or nail their tails down so that the fight will last longer."

A chorus of disbelief broke out and

one or two of the girls pretended to be sick until Mrs Graham said that that would do.

"It's true," said Tilly. "Look, you can read it for yourselves."

They all came to crowd round, except for Cecil, who stayed in his seat.

Tilly warned them to be careful not to tear the paper. "My mum hasn't finished reading it. She'll kill me if I bring it home looking like a dog's breakfast."

"I doubt that, Tilly," said Mrs Graham.

The more the children read, the angrier they got.

"Listen to this!" said Angus. "The police found tunnels had been dug into a sett where they think half a dozen badgers were living. They had all been taken away!"

"It's disgusting," pronounced Megan Montgomery.

Mrs Graham asked what they knew about badgers.

"They're nocturnal," offered William.

"What does that mean?" asked Megan.

"They go out at night," said Cecil, again in his bored voice. The class was beginning to give him frosty looks. "They come out to look for food."

"Do you know what they eat, Cecil?"

Of course he did. "Earthworms and beetles, sometimes baby rabbits and birds. They're carnivorous."

He seems to know an awful lot about badgers, thought Tilly.

Mrs Graham suggested they do a project on badgers and their habitats. They had several books about animals in the classroom and they could also look on the internet. They had acquired a computer just that term.

They discovered that badgers lived

in groups of four to twelve adults, known as clans.

"Just like our clans," said Angus.

"Except they don't wear kilts," said Tilly.

Everybody laughed except Cecil. Well, of course, you wouldn't expect him to laugh at someone else's joke, would you? Tilly thought it likely he wouldn't know any jokes himself.

They had known that badgers lived underground but not that they inhabited such big networks of underground tunnels and chambers. They drew the tunnels and badgers sleeping inside them. Mrs Graham pinned the drawings up round the room and admired each one. William was especially good at drawing. He had won a prize in a national painting competition. But today another drawing stood out. It had been done by

Cecil. When the teacher praised it he said his father was a famous artist.

"What is his name, Cecil? Maybe we'll have heard of him."

"Lancelot Lawson." Cecil did not speak in such a confident tone this time, which was odd, for either he knew his father's name or he didn't.

Tilly's own dad had died when she was a baby but she did know his name and she had a photo of him on her dressing table.

Mrs Graham had obviously not heard of Lancelot Lawson.

"Lancelot!" Billy was sniggering again.

Mrs Graham decided they should move on to something else. As they were going out at breaktime she called Billy back. "Just a moment. I want a word with you."

During the break, Cecil kept to himself. He didn't seem to want to make friends. When William offered him a biscuit he refused, politely enough. At lunchtime, he asked if he could stay in the classroom and read. It was drizzling slightly but the rest of the class, the girls included, went out to play football in the back field.

"Fancies himself, that Silly Cecil," said Billy. "Sss-illy Ccc-ecil." The name was going to stick.

"He might just be shy," suggested Tilly.

"Shy? He's not shy when it comes to opening his mouth. Mr Know-All."

Throughout the day, no matter what they were doing, badgers kept working their way back into Tilly's head. She didn't put the newspaper in her bag at the end of the day. She kept it out so that she could read it again on the way home.

As they were coming out of the school gate they saw an estate car draw up and Cecil hop into the front passenger seat. A woman – his mother, they presumed – was in the driving seat. They had not been able to find out where he lived but it was obviously not in the village itself.

When they called in at the shop Mrs Paterson was able to tell them that the new people were renting a house about three miles away called Laurel Lodge. It was a big house, set well back from the road, screened by high, overgrown fir trees, and had been empty for some time.

"Mrs Lawson was in a few minutes ago."

"The dad's called Lancelot," said Tilly. "Bit of a tongue-twister. Lancelot Lawson."

"Lancelot," repeated Mrs Paterson, frowning. "Name rings a bell but I can't think where."

"Was Mrs Lawson nice?" asked Tilly.

"She was very civil. But she didn't give much away." Mrs Paterson wouldn't have liked that. She relied on people giving things away for her gossip.

Thinking about that, Tilly went on, "You've not heard of anyone mentioning badgers, have you?"

"Badgers? Can't say I have."

When they'd left the shop William said, "You don't think anyone's going to tell Mrs Paterson, do you? It'd be like putting an ad in the *Gazette*."

"You never know," responded Tilly huffily. "Sometimes people can let things slip without meaning to."

"Like you, you mean?"

Tilly stuck her tongue out at him. At times she had been known to open her mouth when it would have been better to keep it zipped up.

They took the short cut across the field and she opened up the newspaper again.

"The Scottish Society for the Prevention of Cruelty to Animals say they need people to come forward with any information they might have about possible badger-baiters."

"Well, we don't have any," said William.

"Not at the moment, anyway," returned Tilly.

CHAPTER 2

"We can't start looking for badger-baiters!" protested William.

He groaned, remembering the trouble they'd landed themselves in when Tilly was on the warpath protecting wild goats. They'd got mixed up in more than they'd bargained for, as William's mother had put it afterwards. For a while things had turned quite nasty. But he was glad they'd done it, though. As well as saving the goats from eviction they had rescued old Mr Sheridan from the clutches of his horrible estate manager and housekeeper. And there were their goats now, a long thin brown line of them, running free in the cleft between the hills, just as their ancestors had done for centuries before them.

"I'm not suggesting we do anything *dangerous*," retorted Tilly. "Anyway, they warn you not to go near anywhere or anyone you suspect but to go straight to the police. So when we find a suspect that's what we'll do."

"You say that as if you think it'd be easy-peasy."

"You don't know till you try, do you?"

"But if the police can't find them?"

Tilly thought for a moment. "They're too busy catching burglars and murderers... A badger-baiter is a kind of murderer, isn't he?"

"Well, I don't think we've got any badger-baiters round here."

"How can you be sure?"

"We know everybody."

"Not *everybody*," insisted Tilly. "Not for miles and *miles* around."

"My dad does." William's dad, Mr Beattie, had a plumbing business so he travelled all over the region regularly.

"He can't possibly. Not every single last person."

"Yes, he can!"

Tilly was on the point of flouncing off but she stopped herself. "All I'm suggesting, William Beattie, is that we keep our eyes and ears open. You want to help save the badgers, don't you?"

"I suppose so."

"You *suppose* so?"

"Yes, I do. Of course I do! It sounds

29

horrible, dogs attacking them."

"Well, then!"

"But how would we go about it?"

"You could start by asking your dad if he's ever come across anything suspicious."

They parted, William to cut across to Bank Cottages, Tilly to carry on towards Sheridan House. She turned and called back to him, "But don't let him know what we're up to!"

"Do you think I would!" William muttered to himself.

He went home knowing that there was no stopping Tilly Trotwood once she'd got a bee in her bonnet.

As he opened the door he was all but knocked over by his dog, Sandy. He took him out for a romp in the back wood and forgot about the business of the badger-baiters but when his dad came in at teatime he thought about it again. He told him about the clipping Tilly had cut out from the newspaper.

"I saw that myself." His dad shook his head. "Bunch of thugs. It's a bad business, no question."

"You've never seen any sign of anything like that going on, have you?"

"Certainly not! If I had do you not think I'd have been onto the police straightaway?"

William knew that was true.

"You'll have a new boy in your class?"

"Cecil?" said William with surprise.

"I've been doing a bit of work at the house they've rented. Plumbing was in a bad way, nothing's been done to it for years. Whole house is the same and the outbuildings are falling to bits. Is the lad OK?"

"Dunno. He's, well, a bit different."

"Wouldn't do if we were all the same. Need to give him a chance."

"He's not very friendly."

"His folks aren't either. Seems they want to keep themselves to themselves. I've only met the lady of the house. The man's never around. The lady's polite enough but she's not got much to say for herself. They've put a PRIVATE sign up at the end of the drive."

After tea, William called Sandy and

went along the road to Tilly's house.

Her mum was sitting at the table with some papers in front of her looking a bit glum. "Hi, William," she said to him absent-mindedly.

"Want to come for a walk with Sandy?" he asked Tilly, who jumped up and fetched her anorak.

They set off up the drive towards the big house.

"What's up with your mum?" he asked.

"She's short of money."

He was surprised that Tilly would even mention it. Her mum was always hard up.

"It's worse than usual," said Tilly.

"So she's decided she needs to expand. Try to get more clients in the town. A lot of folk round here aren't up for reflexology."

William knew his mother wouldn't be interested in having her feet massaged even though his Auntie Netta had tried to encourage her. She had had it done herself and said afterwards that she felt it had done her a power of good. She'd told his mum that she was too stuck in her ways.

"Hey, she could try Cecil's mother!" cried Tilly. "They look as if they've got money. Did you see Cecil's trainers? And they've got an estate car."

"It's quite old though."

"Is it?" Tilly didn't notice these things but William was interested in cars.

"I don't know that she'd get far with Mrs Lawson. My dad seems to think they're all a bit snooty."

They went round to the back door of the big house and rapped on it. Mrs Young, the housekeeper, let them in.

"You must have smelt my baking! I've just taken a batch of jam tarts out of the oven. Plum jam."

"Yummy plummy," said Tilly.

Sandy began to bark and his tail swooshed from side to side.

"All right, Sandy," said Mrs Young, patting his head, "I expect I'll find something for you! We'll take some tarts up for Mr Sheridan too."

She loaded up a tray with tea for Mr Sheridan and juice for them and a large plate of jam tarts.

He was pleased to see them. He'd been sitting in his wheelchair at the window looking through his telescope at the wild goats running in the distance. His eyesight was not very good, which was hardly surprising considering he was more than ninety years old.

He swivelled round when they came in.

"Now sit down, the two of you, and give me all your news!"

He loved to hear what was going on in the village as he didn't get out much himself. Occasionally Mr Young would take him for a run in the car though he always said he was quite happy as long as he could look out of the window. From there he had a big wide view onto the world.

Tilly launched into her badger tale.

"Well, that is an amazing coincidence!" exclaimed Mr Sheridan. "I've been thinking about badgers too, today."

"Telepathy," suggested William.

Only the other day in school Mrs Graham had been telling them that when two people thought the same thing at the same time it was telepathy.

"Not exactly," said Mr Sheridan. "I heard an item on the radio. The S.S.P.C.A. are offering a reward of a thousand pounds to anyone who manages to give information that leads to an arrest and charge."

"A thousand pounds," echoed Tilly and William together.

"My mum could do with a thousand pounds," said Tilly.

"So could mine," rejoined William.

"We could share it," proposed Tilly. "Half each. That would still be five hundred pounds."

"Of course you'd have to to get the information first," put in Mr Sheridan. Tilly saw that he was not taking their proposal seriously. "That wouldn't be easy."

"We could start by making enquiries."

"I don't think it's a good idea, Tilly." Mr Sheridan shook his head. "I doubt if you'd get far and, apart from that, it could be dangerous. So, put it right out of your head!"

But Tilly, being Tilly, had no intention of putting it out of her head. They didn't talk about it any more then. They ate their jam tarts and drank their juice and told Mr Sheridan about the new boy at school. Mr Sheridan had known Laurel Lodge before it had fallen into such a bad state. He wasn't sure who owned it now.

"Perhaps the Lomaxes still do. They were the former owners. They left years ago in a hurry. Must be twenty years. There was a scandal, you see."

"Scandal?" Tilly pricked her ears up.

"Mr Lomax embezzled some money from the bank he worked for and went to prison."

"It's amazing how many interesting things go on round here, isn't it?" said Tilly.

Mr Sheridan smiled. "That is very true. When you look out of the window it all seems very peaceful."

*

On their way back, William and Tilly returned to the subject of badger-baiting. They considered the thousand-pound reward money. That seemed to settle it. They couldn't pass up the chance of that, could they?

"We need to draw up a list of suspects," said Tilly.

"A *list*? We haven't even got one name to put on it."

"What about Silly Cecil's family? They seem a funny lot. *And* they've put a PRIVATE notice at the end of their drive."

"But they've just moved into the district."

"Maybe they moved there because it's so private and out of the way. Nobody would see what was going on."

"They've got outbuildings," mused William.

"You see!"

"Lots of people have outbuildings."

"Well, I think we should investigate them anyway."

"And how are we to do that?"

"I could get my mum to put a reflexology leaflet through their door. Knowing my mum, she'd probably ring the bell and have a chat with Mrs L."

"You can't ask your mum to snoop around."

" 'Course not. We'll go along for the ride and while she's chatting to Mrs L. we can take a little look round."

Before they parted Tilly added, "Don't tell anyone else about the thousand pounds. They'll all be looking for badger-baiters then."

CHAPTER 3

"Do you think Mrs Lawson would be interested in having reflexology?" asked Tilly's mum.

"She drives an estate car, so they must be well-off," said Tilly.

"Not necessarily."

"But they must have more money than us." They themselves had a clapped-out old car that Annabel, Tilly's mum's best friend, had sold to them for next to nothing. It broke down regularly and had just managed to scrape through its M.O.T. test. "You were saying you need more clients."

"I suppose I could give it a go. Anyway, you'd better get a move on. You're cutting it fine yet again!"

Tilly picked up her bag and ran. When she caught up with William she gave him the thumbs-up. "She's going to do it. Come round after school."

The estate car was pulling up outside the school gates as they arrived. The passenger door opened and out hopped Cecil. He didn't look at Tilly and William. His mother waved to him and he waved back and then he walked into the playground, looking neither right nor left.

"Sss-illy Ccc-ecil." That was Billy Black. "Sssssss."

"Sssssss," copied two of the small boys in primary one, who tagged around after Billy. He was their hero because he was good at football.

"Mind you, he's asking for it," muttered Tilly. "Cecil. He could just *try* to be a bit nice."

Even Mrs Graham seemed to be getting annoyed with him. He kept answering questions and making remarks without giving anyone else a chance.

"You must put your hand up first, Cecil," she told him firmly, for the second time.

"In my other school—"

"This is not your other school."

Billy smirked and Tilly couldn't help feeling a little pleased herself at Cecil getting ticked off.

At breaktime Mrs Graham insisted on Cecil going out. "Fresh air will do you good. And some exercise. Don't you like playing football, Cecil?"

"No," he said and went to stand by the school gate.

At the end of the day, he was collected by his mother again.

Tilly walked home with William and he told his mother he was going out with Tilly and her mum for a while. She didn't ask where. She was busy making a new cake recipe and counting out the ingredients.

They had a drink and a biscuit at Tilly's house before setting out.

"I'm really not sure about this," said Tilly's mum.

"Mum, you're only going to put a leaflet through the door. She can't eat you."

"You're right. Come on then, let's go!"

49

Tilly and William jumped into the back of the car and strapped themselves in. The engine started after huffing and puffing a bit. They went through the village and turned off the main road into a minor one. There was hardly ever any traffic on this road. Just the place for secret meetings, thought Tilly, as they chugged along. One thing was certain: her mother would never be able to break the speed limit, not in this car.

"It's just along here," said William, leaning forward.

The entrance to the drive of Laurel Lodge came into view and, along with it, the large notice saying PRIVATE.

"I can't possibly drive in there when it says PRIVATE," declared Tilly's mum, braking hard and coming to a skid, skewed at an angle across the drive entrance. The car shuddered for a moment, and the engine died.

"People must be able to drive in to deliver post and things," said Tilly, releasing herself from her seat belt. "After all, the gates are open." On a closer look, she realised their hinges were broken so they probably wouldn't shut anyway.

Her mum was twisting hard on the starter. The engine coughed, died, and then wouldn't cough again, no matter how much its driver was begging it to.

"Now what am I going to do?" She slapped the steering wheel.

"You could phone Johnny," said William. Johnny was the village mechanic.

"I'll have to!"

It would not be the first time. Johnny was used to rescuing them from all sorts of odd places around the countryside.

Tilly's mum rummaged in her bag until she found her mobile phone. She clicked it on, stared at it and frowned.

"Oh no," she moaned, "it's not possible! The battery's dead."

But it was possible: the phone was quite dead.

"Looks like we're stuck," declared Tilly cheerfully. She was thinking that this might be a good place to be stuck, as far as their investigations were concerned. "We could go up to the house and ask to use their phone." She already had the car door open.

"I guess we've no other option. There isn't a phone box for miles."

"Nearest one is in the village," said William.

"Not much use that, is it?"

They set off up the drive, with Tilly in the middle. What a piece of luck! She felt like skipping. Big trees overhung the path, making it feel kind of creepy. She remarked on that but her mother was too busy striding along thinking about her broken-down car to even notice.

The trees opened out and there, ahead, stood the house. It was not as big as Sheridan House but it was quite large, nevertheless. William saw what his father had meant about the place being run down. The windows needed painting and the gutters sagged. The walls were blotched with dark stains where leaks had run down the stones.

"Wouldn't fancy living there." Tilly's mum wrinkled her nose. "I don't suppose they plan to stay long. Maybe just till they find something better."

She climbed the broken steps to the front door, taking care not to trip, with Tilly and William close on her heels. After glancing around she lifted the heavy black wrought-iron door knocker and knocked twice. They waited.

Meanwhile, Tilly was scanning the weed-choked gardens. There was no sign of outhouses. They must be round the back.

"They might not be in." Her mum tried again.

This time, they heard footsteps and then the sound of the door being tugged open. On the step, facing them, was Cecil.

"Hi, Cecil!" cried Tilly. "We've broken down. Just outside your gate."

He looked horrified.

"Is your mum in?" asked Tilly's mum.

He nodded and vanished into the darkness behind the door. A minute or two later Mrs Lawson appeared. She looked flustered.

"I'm terribly sorry to bother you. I'm Tanya Trotwood, by the way."

Tilly's mum held out her hand and Cecil's mother took it. "I wonder if I could possibly use your phone? We've broken down in the road outside and my mobile's not working."

"Oh yes, yes, of course." Mrs Lawson stepped back to allow Tilly's mum to come in. She looked uncertainly at Tilly and William.

"We'll just wait out here," said Tilly.

The door closed behind the two women.

"Let's go round the back." Tilly was already on the way.

They found the estate car parked in the yard behind the house.

"Look, outbuildings!" Tilly headed for the biggest one, a large corrugated-roofed barn. The roof, like everything else, was in need of repair. Hadn't the report in the *Gazette* talked about badger-baiting being held in barns?

"Be careful!" cautioned William. "You never know what might be in there." He was thinking of vicious dogs.

58

Tilly had her hand on the door when, suddenly, it opened, right in her face. She stepped back just in time to stop it hitting her on the nose. Facing her was a man, frowning heavily under thick black brows. She wondered if he could be Cecil's father but he didn't look much like an artist. He was wearing overalls and he looked grubby.

"What are you doing here?" he barked.

"My mum's using the telephone." Tilly started to gabble about cars and engines and mobile phones. Then she stopped short, realising that all of that had nothing to do with snooping in other people's barns. "We were just, sort of, interested. In case you had any cows. Or pigs," she added lamely.

"We don't keep cows or pigs," he said abruptly.

He pulled the door shut behind him before Tilly could get a glimpse of what was inside. He ushered them back across the yard.

"Cecil's in our class at school," offered Tilly.

He made no comment.

"I expect my mum will be out in a minute."

He left them without a word and

went into the house by the back door.

"I see what my dad meant about them not being friendly," said William.

Tilly's mum was taking rather a long time.

"I hope she's all right," said Tilly uneasily.

"They're not going to hit her on the head and tie her up, are they?"

"You never know."

"Don't be so daft!"

Eventually the front door opened and out came Tilly's mum, calling back her thanks to Cecil's mother and saying, "I'll see you on Wednesday then, Margo!"

See you on Wednesday! Margo! What was going on?

"Johnny should be here by now," said Tilly's mum. "He said he'd come straightaway. I don't know what I'd do without him."

She set off at a trot down the drive. Tilly and William had to run to catch up with her.

"Mum, what was all that about seeing Mrs Lawson on Wednesday?"

"She's going to have a reflexology session with me."

"*She's what?*"

"I took the opportunity to give her my leaflet and told her that reflexology was a great stress-buster. And she said she had a lot of stress that needed busting! I'd thought she seemed very tense."

"So she can afford it?"

"Not really. It seems they are quite

hard up. I'm doing it for half price."

"Hard up? But what about Cecil's trainers?"

"I expect she wanted him to go to his new school looking smart. You see, Tilly, you shouldn't make your mind up too quickly about people."

They could see the bottom of the drive now and there was Johnny standing by their car with the hood up. They waved to him.

"She's actually very nice," said Tilly's mum. "Her name's Margo."

"I thought it must be," said Tilly. "Did she ask you to call her Margo?"

"She softened once I started to talk to her. I've a feeling she needs a friend."

It was said in the village that Tanya Trotwood could talk to anyone, like her daughter. William grinned.

"So, are you going to go to her house?" asked Tilly.

"No, I offered to. But she said she'd rather come to me."

That was a pity, thought Tilly. Still, you never knew what her mum might find out once she had Cecil's mother lying on her plinth for an hour.

CHAPTER 4

It was Wednesday afternoon and Cecil was waiting for his mother to come and pick him up after her reflexology session with Tilly's mother.

He was hovering around the school gate. His mother was late. Tilly wasn't surprised. Her mum often over-ran with her clients.

Cecil was beginning to look anxious. He kept peering along the road and in between times he paced up and down. Tilly went over to him.

"I'm sure she'll be along soon. It's just that my mum, once she gets talking, forgets about time. Has your dad painted any good pictures recently?"

Cecil shrugged. "One or two."

"Does he spend all his time painting?"

"Quite a lot."

Getting information out of Cecil was like getting blood out of a stone.

Tilly hoped her mother had been having more luck with his mother, who was arriving now.

"Hello, dear," Mrs Lawson greeted Tilly when she pulled up.

"Did you have a nice time with my mum?"

"Yes, thank you."

They drove off and Tilly hurried home with William.

"Did she say anything?" Tilly asked her mum at once. "Mrs Lawson?"

"How do you mean, *say* anything? We talked. She's unhappy, the poor woman, but she didn't tell me about what, not outright. Something to do with her husband, though. And Cecil."

"Cecil?" repeated William.

"He's not happy at school."

Tilly and William thought they might be able to tell her why. Cecil was having a rough time but he wasn't doing much to help himself. He kept trying to show off. He thought he knew more than any of them about everything. Sometimes they felt sorry for him but when they tried to talk to him he shunned them.

"I told her it takes a while for kids to adapt to a new place," said Tilly's mum. Then she noticed something lying on the chair. "That's her bag. She's left it!"

"We could take it along on our bikes," offered Tilly, reaching for the bag.

"Well," said her mum doubtfully, "I'm not sure. I don't like you cycling so far."

"It's only three miles, and we'll be very careful."

"I'd go myself but my next client's due in five minutes."

"We'll do it, won't we, William?"

"Yes, sure."

"Ask your mum first, though, William," Tilly's mum called after them, adding, "And get a carton of milk at the shop on your way back, Tilly. We're almost out."

William's mother said, "All right, but don't be long. And make sure you keep into the side of the road."

They promised.

Sandy was annoyed at being left behind but they couldn't take him. He barked loudly at them as they took off.

They covered the three miles quite quickly. When they got to the house, they bumped their way up the rough drive, avoiding the worst of the potholes. Tilly went through one that had muddy water in it and got her legs splashed. She was still wearing her school trousers. Her mother would not be pleased.

They dropped their bikes in the grass in front of the house and went up the steps to the main door. They knocked, but nobody came so they decided to try round the back.

As they rounded the corner of the house they heard voices, raised voices. They were coming from the big barn. They moved closer. It sounded as if Mr and Mrs Lawson were having a row.

"I can't put up with this much longer, Lance," Mrs Lawson was saying. "It's no way to live."

Mr Lawson muttered something too low for them to hear. They crept away, feeling that maybe they shouldn't be listening to this after all. Tilly knew her mum would be furious if she could see her. Her mum liked to pick up gossip but she said you shouldn't eavesdrop. That was sneaky.

*

On the way home they stopped off at the shop. William's Auntie Netta was at the counter blethering to Mrs Paterson.

"Awful business, isn't it?" Auntie Netta was saying.

"It certainly is," agreed Mrs Paterson. "You were asking me about badgers just the other day, Tilly."

"Why, what's up?"

"The police found three this morning. Their carcasses, that is. They were dead. They'd been dumped in a pit a couple of miles along the back road."

"They'd been mauled, by dogs," said Auntie Netta. "So it seems anyway."

Tilly and William gave each other a long look.

"Have the police any idea who did it?" asked William.

"Apparently not. They think the badgers were probably dumped there in the middle of the night."

"We've never had anything like that happen round here before, have we?" said Mrs Paterson.

The door pinged open and in came Mrs Mackie, the postie's wife, followed by Mrs Flynn, the janitor's wife.

"Have you heard the news?" they cried. "About the badgers?"

"News travels fast," observed Auntie Netta, who was good at helping it along herself.

The next moment, the door opened again and in puffed Mrs Ewbank, whom Tilly and William called the Ewe, though not to her face, of course. Shewas quite a large lady and took up a good deal of room. By this time the shop was crowded. Tilly and William had to move up.

"I don't know what the place is coming to!" declared the Ewe. "Imagine, we have badger-baiters in our midst!"

A chorus rang out.

"Isn't it dreadful?"

"Frightful!"

"Disgusting!"

When the noise had subsided

Mrs Flynn said, "It must be strangers to the district," and everyone agreed.

Mrs Paterson, with a glance at the clock, announced it was time she shut up shop. "So if anyone is wanting anything?"

"Your mum's milk, Tilly." William nudged her.

She had forgotten, with all the fuss going on. She bought the milk and they escaped before the rush to leave.

They jumped back on their bikes and cycled home, Tilly leaving William at his gate. It was only when she was wheeling her bike into the shed behind her house that she remembered that she hadn't delivered Mrs Lawson's bag! It was still in her saddle bag. She went into the house carrying it.

"Mum," she began before her mother could start, "I'm sorry, really I am, but I forgot to give Mrs Lawson her bag."

"You forgot? But that's what you went for!"

"I know. But I *couldn't* give it to her."

"Why ever not? Was she not in?"

"Well, she was, sort of. She was in the barn with Mr Lawson. And they were having an awful row. I couldn't go barging in, could I?"

"No, certainly not. Oh well, she'll know where it is at any rate."

When Tilly told her mum about the badgers she was as horrified as everyone else.

They were in the middle of their meal when the police arrived. They'd come from the station in the town as there wasn't one in the village any more. There were two of them, a man, PC Cairns, and a woman, WPC Robertson. They were making house-to-house enquiries about the badgers.

They apologised for disturbing.

"That's all right," said Tilly's mum. "It's a sorry business. Would you like a cup of tea?"

The police officers accepted and drank while they wrote in their notebooks, not that Tilly and her mum were able to give them much to write. Tilly wondered for a moment if she could tell them about her suspicions but only for a moment. They'd have to get more evidence, she and William, before they could confide in the police.

"If you do hear or see anything suspicious let us know," the constables said as they prepared to leave and continue up the drive to Sheridan House.

"Of course!" said Tilly and her mum.

Tilly had not long gone to bed and was reading, something she always did before she fell asleep, when the doorbell rang. She perked up her ears, heard her mum go to the door and then say, "Oh, come on in, Margo! Have you come for your bag?"

The door closed and the two women went into the sitting room, which was opposite Tilly's bedroom. They must not have closed the door properly as their voices could be heard easily. Her mum offered Margo a cup of tea.

"That would be very nice, Tanya. I could do with a break, I have to confess."

"Feeling a bit low, are you?"

"You could say that!"

"Do you want to talk?"

"Oh, it's just I hate that house!" Mrs Lawson spoke vehemently, which made Tilly sit up straight instead of slouching against the pillows. She could understand hating the house. Maybe the ghosts of those people, the Lomaxes, were still haunting it.

"It is a bit bleak," agreed Tilly's mum.

"I wish we didn't have to live there but we've got no choice."

"You don't *have* to stay, do you?"

"I'm afraid we do."

Tilly wondered why but Mrs Lawson changed the subject and started to ask about the nearest town

and its facilities. She said she'd like to find a job and that she used to work as a dental assistant. Tilly's mum sounded doubtful about her finding anything in the town. There was only one dentist and he already had an assistant.

Tilly put out her light, thinking about Laurel Lodge and the Lawsons. There was definitely something wrong with the place. Perhaps Mr Lawson was running badger-baiting contests in the barn and Mrs Lawson, although she loathed the whole idea, could do nothing to stop him. She could hardly tell on her own husband to the police. The more Tilly thought about it, the more it seemed to be a possibility. After all, there hadn't been any badger-baiting going on in their area – not that they knew of, at least – until the Lawson family arrived on the scene.

CHAPTER 5

Tilly and William had a meeting to discuss progress so far. They agreed that they seemed to have arrived at a stalemate and were not sure what to do next. Investigating the Lawsons' barn would be the obvious thing but that would not be easy. It would only be possible if the family were to go away but they appeared always to be around.

"Do you ever go away for the

weekend?" Tilly asked Cecil in school the following morning.

He looked startled. "The weekend? No."

"Have you not got any relations? A granny or grandpa, or aunts and uncles?" She didn't have many herself, only an aunt and uncle and their children, and they lived in England. That was why she called William's relatives aunts and uncles. And Mr Sheridan was like a grandpa to her.

"I've got an uncle who lives in Yorkshire," Cecil answered reluctantly. He clearly did not like being interrogated.

"That's where my aunt and uncle live!" cried Tilly. "Maybe they know each other?"

"Hardly!" Cecil was recovering his superior tone of voice. "It's a big place, Yorkshire."

"Where do they live?"

"Near Harrogate."

Tilly was not sure where that was. "Mine live in Bradford."

Cecil showed no interest.

"Are you not planning to visit your uncle?"

He shook his head.

"You must go on holiday sometime," insisted Tilly.

He shrugged.

She left it. She was getting nowhere.

After school, she and William decided to set down everything they knew in notebooks.

"Like the police do," said Tilly. "It might help us to think better."

They bought notebooks in the shop. Tilly got one with a basket of kittens on the front and William chose one with a dog. They then went to William's house to write their notes.

Tilly put down everything she knew about Cecil and his family, including the fact that he had an uncle in Yorkshire.

"What's that got to do with it?" asked William.

"You never know, he might be into badger-baiting too. He might be part of a chain."

"We need more suspects. After all, it might not be Mr Lawson. How would he get set up so quickly when he'd just come to live here?"

"He could if he was part of a chain. A bigger organisation."

"You've got too much imagination, Tilly Trotwood." William had heard her mum telling her that.

"You can't have too much." Tilly returned to the subject of Mr Lawson. "He might have been doing it in their last place so he'd have contacts."

"Might," said William. "We need some facts."

Next day, Tilly asked Cecil where he used to live.

"Why do you want to know?"

"Just wondered."

"It's none of your business!" He put his back to her and marched off. As he crossed the playground a fast-moving football narrowly missed his ankles. He'd had to jump aside. "Ssss..." went the sniggers.

"Lay off, you lot!" shouted Tilly but Billy and his pals just grinned. When Cecil's mother collected him after school she waved to Tilly and William. They waved back though Cecil ignored them.

That afternoon, Tilly got a bit of a "break", as she thought of it. The way the police sometimes did. When she arrived home from school her mum said she had to go to Laurel Lodge to give Mrs Lawson a treatment. "Mr Lawson is taking the car to Edinburgh so she can't come to me. So you'll either have to come with me or go to William's."

Tilly opted straightaway for going to Laurel Lodge!

"You're sure now? I know you don't like Cecil much."

"Sure."

"You can take a book with you."

Tilly took one, and her notebook and a pencil. She thought she might like to join the police when she grew up, and be a detective. When they passed William's house on the way she wished she could run in and tell him where she was going. He would be surprised!

There was no sign of Cecil when they arrived at Laurel Lodge. The house was so big he could be anywhere. Mrs Lawson showed Tilly into the sitting room.

"Just make yourself at home, dear."

"Thank you," said Tilly.

She didn't think she could ever feel at home here. The room smelt musty, like it had been shut up for a long while. And it was chilly, with only an ancient-looking, two-bar electric fire for heating. But she was happy. She was to be left alone, for a whole hour! Mrs Lawson said they would be at the end of the corridor should she need them, and went out, shutting the door behind her.

Tilly listened to her footsteps fading away. The house was quiet now except for a few odd creaks. She didn't think she'd like to be left on her own here at night.

She examined the room. A big, saggy settee and two armchairs were drawn up in a half-circle round the fire so that you could keep your legs warm at least. The roses on the sofa and seat covers had all but faded away.

The rest of the furniture was big and heavy and treacle-brown in colour. She preferred the nice bright colours they had in their own living room.

The pictures on the walls had gilt frames and were mostly of people. Dead ancestors, she presumed. She and her mum sometimes visited old houses that were open to the public and they had lots of those kind of paintings. Mr Sheridan did too.

She moved on to the bookcase, which covered one wall and stretched right up to the ceiling. The books were old and dusty. There wouldn't be any clues there. She went over to the table with the fancy curved legs standing in front of the window. It had a single drawer. After taking a quick glance over her shoulder she inched it open. Lying in the bottom was a book. An album. Carefully she lifted it out and laid it on top of the table. It had thin sheets of tissue paper between the leaves and, like everything else, was dusty. She turned a page. The photographs were all of Lomaxes. Their names were written below each one. One photograph caught her eye. "Henry Lomax," she read. He looked like Cecil!

"What are you doing?"

She jumped, nearly out of her skin, as she told William later, and he said she would look funny without skin, rattling around like a skeleton. But this was not a funny moment for her.

Cecil was standing in the doorway.

She could not think what to say, which did not happen often to her. She felt her face grow red-hot.

"What are you doing with that?" Cecil came striding towards her.

"I was just looking at the pictures," she faltered.

"You've no right to be poking around in our things!"

She knew that, though she wondered why he should be so annoyed when she had only been looking at an old photograph album. They weren't even photos of his family. She stood to the side and let him close the book and return it to its place in the drawer.

"I wasn't doing any harm. I was being careful, really I was. I wasn't going to steal anything."

"My father would be angry."

Tilly thought it was fortunate that he had gone to Edinburgh. And his mother should be in a good mood after a session with her mum.

Cecil was saying nothing now. He had closed up again, the way he did in the school playground.

She looked at the large picture of a man in a wig at the side of the fireplace.

"Don't suppose you know who any of these people are?"

"Why should I?" he demanded.

"I just wondered."

He showed no sign of leaving and she didn't fancy staying in the room with him. He had moved over to the middle, where he was standing like a sentry on guard.

"I think I'll go out for a walk," she said.

She sidled past him but as she reached the door, something fell from her pocket. She turned to retrieve it but before she could Cecil pounced. It was her notebook. With all those notes about Cecil himself! He was holding it aloft, above her head. He was a lot taller than she was.

"That's mine," she cried, lunging towards him. He side-stepped and she almost fell over.

"How do I know that? You might have taken it out of the drawer."

He couldn't really think that. It was brand new and everything else in the room was old. He just wanted to taunt her. He was waving it around in the air like a flag.

"Give it to me!"

"I want to see what's in it first."

"You've no right to!"

"You'd no right to look in our drawer."

She went for him again and this time she kicked him in the shins, not too hard, but enough. As she said to William afterwards, she had to, for Cecil wasn't going to give in and it would have been a disaster if he'd read the notes. He yelped and doubled up and let his arm drop. She grabbed the notebook and ran like mad along the corridor, down the stairs and out into the grounds.

Once she'd caught her breath she

went round the back to the yard, limping a little. She'd stubbed her toe, on Cecil's shin.

The estate car was gone and it was a long drive to Edinburgh and back so Mr Lawson would be out of the way for a while. This was her chance to check out the big barn. She'd do it quickly before Cecil decided to come after her.

She went over to the barn and came to a dead halt. It was locked, with a great big heavy padlock. She tugged on it but it wasn't going to give. Foiled again. She stamped her foot in frustration, forgetting she had a sore toe.

CHAPTER 6

"It doesn't prove anything just because it was padlocked," protested William.

"It must mean he's got something to hide," retorted Tilly. "People don't usually lock their barns."

"Unless there's something valuable inside."

"Exactly."

"Well, he can't have a pack of dogs. You'd hear them."

"The people that go along to

badger-baiting might bring their own dogs. Hey, slow down a bit!"

"Your toe hurting you?" William grinned.

Tilly was not going to respond to that one. It was not actually hurting much at all as her mum had put arnica cream on it.

They were walking up the drive to Sheridan House on their way to visit Mr Sheridan. Sandy was with them, trotting along happily at their heels and taking occasional dives into the long grass to investigate the undergrowth. They couldn't ever imagine Sandy attacking a badger. He sometimes chased the Ewe's cat but only after she had been having a go at him, and he stopped when they shouted at him.

William still thought they needed to consider other suspects.

"But where are we to get them from?" demanded Tilly. "Can you think of any?"

"Not really," he admitted.

Today, it was chocolate brownies that Mrs Young had been making. Mr Young was sitting in the kitchen eating one with a cup of tea when they arrived and he was able to vouch for them being good.

"Delicious," he declared, taking another bite. "So what have you two scallywags been up to?"

"Nothing much," answered Tilly. "Did the police come and see you about the badger-baiters?"

"They did. There was nothing much I could tell them, though. I said I'd keep my eyes and ears open." Being an estate manager, Mr Young was out and about a lot.

"It's amazing how well they conceal themselves," said Mrs Young, putting some brownies on a plate for William and Tilly. "Do you want to take them to Mr Sheridan?"

He was dozing in his chair when they went up but he started awake and was pleased to see them.

"I haven't seen you for a day or two. Have you been busy?"

"Quite busy," said Tilly.

"Seen any more of the people in Laurel Lodge?"

Mr Sheridan was very interested in the Lomax family and sad that he'd lost touch with them. Tilly told him about her visit to the house but left out the part about opening the drawer to get the photograph album out.

"I know that Henry Lomax committed a very bad crime, taking other people's money," said Mr Sheridan, "but he was not really a bad man, not in the sense of being *wicked*."

"Why did he do it then?"

"He'd been under great pressure financially so I suppose he was tempted and he fell. And he paid for it by going to prison."

Meanwhile, William was at the window looking through Mr Sheridan's telescope for the goats.

"There they are!" he cried, then added more quietly, "I can see something else. At least I think I can." It was just beginning to get dark so he

could not be absolutely sure. But he did have very sharp eyes.

"What can you see?" asked Tilly.

"Looks like an animal running, quite a big animal, not a rabbit or a hare. And there are two dogs chasing it."

Tilly leapt to her feet. "Let me see!" William swung the telescope round for her. "I can't see anything," she moaned.

"Look near the fold of the hills."

"I see them! I see them! William, do you think it could be a badger?"

William took the telescope again. "I think it could be! The dogs are on it now."

"Oh, no!" cried Tilly.

"And I can see two men standing by." William continued to watch. "The dogs are running back to the men. They must have called them off."

"And the badger?"

"I can't see very clearly. It might be on the ground. There goes one of the men. He's bending down. Now he's dragging something. I can't see them any more."

"Badger-baiters!" shouted Tilly.

"Now you can't be sure of that," warned Mr Sheridan. "The light's too poor."

William asked him if he had a map.

"Of the area, do you mean?"

William nodded.

"Yes, I should have. Let me think." Mr Sheridan rolled himself over to the bureau and let down the folding lid. Tilly and William hovered excitedly behind him. "No, it wouldn't be here. I think it must be in my study."

They set off along the corridor to Mr Sheridan's study, with William pushing his chair.

"Try that cupboard, the one over there by the wall."

They tried it and there were maps in it, heaps of them. They began to sort them out.

"It will be an Ordnance Survey map," Mr Sheridan told them. "An old one. I remember it clearly now. I used to take it with me when I went walking in the hills. Sometimes I went with Henry Lomax."

Ordnance Survey maps gave a lot more detail of the landscape than ordinary maps.

William put his hand on it first. He liked maps and was good at reading them. He had done some orienteering with his dad.

They returned to the sitting room, and the telescope.

"Now," said William, opening out the map, "let's see if we can find where that part is on the map."

He traced his finger along the lines, took a squint through the telescope, and went back to the map again.

"Well?" demanded Tilly. She could hardly contain herself from jumping up and down.

"I *think* I see where it should be," said William cautiously.

"I think we might be on to them!" cried Tilly excitedly.

"Now you must *not* jump to conclusions." Mr Sheridan repeated his warning.

Tilly had, of course, already jumped to them.

"Can we borrow the map?" asked William. "We'll take care of it."

"Of course," said Mr Sheridan.

As they were leaving, he said to them, "Now don't go looking for them!

That *would* be dangerous. And you haven't enough evidence. Come back tomorrow afternoon and we'll keep watch again with the telescope."

He didn't ask them to promise him, which was good, thought Tilly.

After they left him she asked William if he thought he could find the place with the help of the map.

"Possibly."

"Is it near Laurel Lodge?"

"No, it's up a different road."

She felt a bit disappointed about that. Still, it didn't prove anything, one way or the other.

"We must go there, William!"

"Not now, though!"

It was getting dark and their

mothers would be wondering where they were. They should have been home half an hour or so ago.

"Tomorrow then," said Tilly.

William slid Mr Sheridan's Ordnance Survey map into a plastic cover before tucking it into his saddle bag. Being old, it was fragile, and he didn't want to damage it in any way. He tapped his pocket, checking that he had his mini binoculars, and they set off.

The road was an even smaller one than that leading to Laurel Lodge and after a mile or so it became a single track with passing places. They met only one car, a Range Rover, with two men in the front. They waited at the passing place for it to go by but it slowed and the driver put the window down to speak to them. They had never seen either him or his passenger before.

In the back of the car, behind a wire screen, were three fierce-looking dogs.

"Where are you two going?"

"We're just out for a cycle ride." It was Tilly who answered.

"It's a private road further up."

"We won't go there."

"Make sure you don't. We don't like trespassers."

"I didn't like the look of them," said Tilly after they had driven off.

"Or their dogs," added William. "They were lurchers crossed with pit bulls."

"*What!*" Tilly almost fell off her bike. "They could be our badger-baiters."

"Well, they *might* be. But not necessarily."

The men and the dogs had unnerved them a little. They knew they shouldn't be up this lonely road on their own. Everybody would be angry if they found out. Tilly's mum thought she was at William's and his mum thought he was at Tilly's.

"I've got my mum's mobile with me," said Tilly, tapping her pocket.

It had come in useful before when they had run up against the crooks who were ripping off Mr Sheridan.

"I hope we won't need it this time."

When they reached the gate across

the road with a PRIVATE sign they stopped. The gate was locked.

"I don't think we should go any further," said William.

Tilly nodded. It was disappointing but to go on might be too dangerous, even she could see that.

They leant on the gate and gazed up the long, narrow drive that wound its way between the moors until it disappeared. William took out his binoculars.

"There are some kind of buildings up there. They look sort of tumbledown." Then he cocked his head. "I can hear dogs yapping. Sound like terriers." He listened again and this time he heard a car. "Quick, Tilly, it could be the men coming back! Let's hide in the trees!"

They plunged straight into the thick clump of conifers at the side of the road, dragging their bikes behind them. They crouched down low and waited, watching through a narrow gap in the trees.

The Range Rover came into sight and stopped. The driver got out to unlock the gate. The men must have been very anxious about security to have locked it when they'd been gone for such a short time.

The driver had left the car door open and was continuing a conversation with the other man.

"We'll take the terriers out tonight. I've a good idea where there's another sett."

Tilly gasped aloud and clapped a hand over her mouth.

CHAPTER 7

Fortunately for Tilly, the men hadn't heard her. The car engine was still running.

The driver got back in, drove through the opening and pulled up. This time the passenger got out to close the gate. They took off again. Tilly and William stayed in their hiding place until not even the faintest whisper of the car engine could be heard. William crawled out first. He scanned the horizon.

"All clear!"

They cycled home faster than they could ever remember cycling before, bumping over ruts and splashing through puddles, stopping only when they reached the outskirts of the village.

"What'll we do now?" asked Tilly, once she'd ceased puffing. "Tell the police?" It was too far to cycle to the town so they'd have to phone.

"Let's go and talk to Mr Sheridan first," said William.

Mr Sheridan was cross with them to start with, but then he praised them for being sensible and turning back when they did.

"We're not totally stupid," said Tilly with a grin, and he laughed.

"The next step is to telephone the police," he said. "I'll do it for you. I can't believe, though, that they wouldn't have gone up there already to look around."

He rang the police and they said they would be along in an hour. Mr Sheridan suggested that Tilly and William should phone their mothers and ask if they could stay to tea with him. He was sure that Mrs Young wouldn't mind. She liked having young people about the house, as he did himself.

Mrs Young made them some very nice toasted sandwiches with cheese and tomato fillings on wholemeal bread that she had baked herself.

"Isn't she a treasure?" beamed Mr Sheridan as she set down the sandwiches in front of them.

"And there are pancakes with lemon to follow," she said with a smile. She knew that Tilly was fond of pancakes.

They had just finished eating when PC Cairns and WPC Robertson arrived.

They sat down facing William and Tilly. "So what have you got to tell us?"

They told the story between them, Tilly allowing William to get his piece in. Her mum was always telling her to

give other people a chance to open their mouths. The constables cross-questioned them.

"You're quite sure you heard the man saying the word *sett*?"

They were both sure.

"You couldn't have imagined it?"

They shook their heads.

"Can you describe the men?"

They did their best and WPC Robertson wrote down the details.

"You didn't happen to notice the number of the car?"

They had not. William was annoyed with himself for not thinking to do that.

"We thought you must have been out there already?" put in Mr Sheridan.

"Oh, we have. It was deserted."

"It's not deserted now," said William.

"Seems not. We'll put a watch on them until we see some signs of activity. Then we'll go in. But we could go out there and find only the men and the dogs but no badgers. We have to find a badger on the premises before we can make an arrest."

Tilly wished they could be taken along but knew there was not the remotest chance of that so there was no point in asking.

"Now you children must say absolutely *nothing* to anyone about this," said PC Cairns. "You understand?

They mustn't get wind of the fact that we're on to them. We'll take you home and have a word with your parents."

When Tilly's mum saw her coming in with the two police constables she almost fainted.

"Tilly, what on earth have you been doing?"

"It's all right, Mrs Trotwood, no cause for alarm!"

She recovered once they'd explained what was going on, but after they'd gone, taking William with them, she said to Tilly, "I knew you were up to something. Why can you never mind your own business? Those men could be dangerous, with those nasty dogs."

"But, Mum, what if they catch the badger-baiters? You want them to be caught, don't you?"

"Of course. But I'd rather someone else had been doing the catching."

"We didn't go anywhere near them. We just observed them, from a safe distance."

Her mum shook her head.

"And you'd like five hundred pounds, wouldn't you?"

"Just let's wait and see what happens before we start counting the money!"

*

In the morning, Tilly kept wanting to blurt out their secret, but knew she must not. She only went so far as to hint to Kirsty and Megan that she and William had a secret, but nothing more, even though they pestered her to tell them.

Cecil arrived at school smiling!

It was so unusual that everybody gawked and even Billy forgot to make his hissing snake sound.

When Mrs Graham asked if anyone had news, Cecil's hand went straight up.

"My father's going to have an exhibition in London."

"Of his paintings?"

"Yes. About thirty."

"He must have been working very hard?"

"Oh, he has. Very hard."

"That's excellent, Cecil," said Mrs Graham. "He must be good, too, to get an exhibition in London. Has he had one before?"

"Not for a long time."

Tilly shifted uncomfortably on her chair. She had still not totally ruled out Mr Lawson being involved in the badger-baiting gang. But now it seemed that all that had been going on in the barn was painting pictures. Unless they had been a cover-up? Maybe she was letting her imagination run away with itself. She avoided William's eye.

They didn't have a chance to talk at break so they had to wait till lunchtime when they were on their way home. They were having a half-day as Mrs Graham and Miss Todd, the little ones' teacher, had to go to a conference about reading.

"I never did think Mr Lawson had badgers in his barn," said William.

"You're so smart!" Tilly tossed her head.

"Cecil seems terribly pleased about his dad."

Tilly was to find out why when she got home. Mrs Lawson had been in to see her mum that morning and poured out the whole family history. Tilly rang William.

"Come round as soon as you can! I've got something to tell you."

William was round in ten minutes. Tilly was waiting for him at the door.

"We're going up to see Mr Sheridan. He'll want to hear the story too."

"Come on, tell me now! Don't be a meanie!"

"I don't want to tell it twice."

William was sure she would tell it more than once. However, she would not change her mind and he had to wait until they were sitting down with Mr Sheridan.

"You know Cecil, the boy we've told you about?" Tilly began.

Mr Sheridan nodded.

"Well, his father is the son of your friend Mr Lomax." Tilly sat back to enjoy her listeners' surprise.

"Henry Lomax?"

"That's right. When I saw his photo in the album he reminded me of someone. It was Cecil!"

"So Cecil is the grandson of Henry Lomax!"

"He's dead now. Henry Lomax, not Cecil. He died of remorse, so Mrs Lawson told my mum. After he went to prison the family decided to change its name to Lawson."

"So Laurel Lodge actually belongs to the Lawsons? Now tell us the rest of the story, Tilly!"

The Lawsons, apparently, had been having a hard time. Mr Lawson had not been able to sell his work and they'd had to give up their house in Yorkshire because they couldn't pay the mortgage. Laurel Lodge was standing empty so they decided to come and live there.

"Even though Cecil's dad hated the idea," added Tilly.

"Lancelot, or Lance, as we called him, lived there as a child, you see," said Mr Sheridan. "He was a sensitive boy. He would remember the family's disgrace."

"I expect that's why he's been in such a bad mood," said William.

Tilly nodded. "And because he wasn't earning any money. That was getting him down. But now that he's going to have an exhibition in London he's perked up. Cecil's mum told my mum that he's a changed man."

"This is all very interesting indeed," said Mr Sheridan. "I shall invite them to visit me. You must both come and help keep Cecil company."

William shrugged. "I don't know that he likes us very much."

"My mum says we've to start being nice to him," said Tilly. "She says he's been baited in school. A bit like badgers are. Not as badly, though. Nobody really wanted to hurt him."

"I should hope not!" said Mr Sheridan.

There was a tap on the door and Mrs Young looked in. "Visitors for you," she announced.

She ushered in PC Cairns and WPC Robertson and another man, a stranger to them. He turned out to be from the S.S.P.C.A.

"We've been looking for you two," said the woman constable. "We were told you'd be here."

"We've got some news for you," said PC Cairns. "We caught the badger-baiters last night. In the act."

William and Tilly whooped and Mr Sheridan beamed.

"Sit down, please," he invited. "Do tell us everything!"

The constables seated themselves.

They – along with two others for back-up – had arrested four men and taken their dogs into custody. They had found one dead badger and another so badly mauled that they'd had to put it down.

The man from the S.S.P.C.A. then explained how the terriers rooted out badgers. When the men found what they thought was an entrance to a sett they fastened a little transmitter to the dog's neck and sent it down. Up on the ground they had a receiver so that they could hear what was going on below.

Once the dog located a sett they dug down and the badgers came out and tried to escape. And at that point the men let the lurcher-cum-pit bulls loose on them.

"What a horrible tale!" said Mr Sheridan. "But at least those particular men won't be doing it again."

"Thanks to you, Tilly and William!" said WPC Robertson. "So, well done!"

"Will we get the reward now?" Tilly couldn't keep the question back any

longer. "The thousand pounds?"

The man from the S.S.P.C.A. smiled. "It may take a little while to process but, yes, you will. The men have been arrested and charged. That is all we need."

The visitors rose, promising to keep in touch. They said they'd see themselves out.

"What are you going to do with your money?" Tilly asked William as soon as the door closed behind them.

CHAPTER 8

Mr Sheridan gave a small party for the Lawsons. A welcome-home party, as he put it. A little delayed, but better late than never. Tilly came with her mum and William with his mum and dad. His dad had known Cecil's dad as a boy. Mr and Mrs Young were also invited to join them. She had made some delicious tartlets and sausage rolls for the occasion as well as a selection of cream cakes. The grown-ups drank fizzy wine and the children had pineapple juice with sparkling water.

Mr Sheridan proposed a toast. "Welcome home, Lance! And a warm welcome to Margo and Cecil, too!"

They raised their glasses and drank.

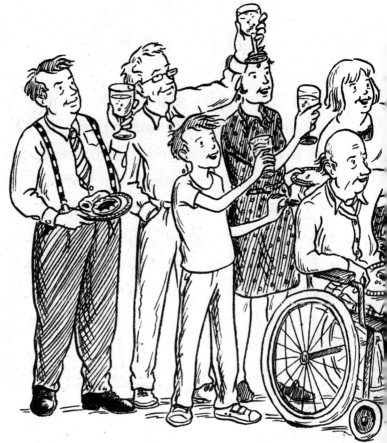

All three Lawsons were smiling. Cecil's mum had told Tilly's mum that when they got some money they were going to decorate Laurel Lodge. She thought that after that they would grow to like the house much more. She already did. They planned to stay and make it their home.

Tilly and William were keeping Cecil company, as Mr Sheridan wished them to do.

"That was fantastic, you catching the badger-baiters!" Cecil shook his head in admiration. "It was very brave of you."

Tilly was beginning to think he might not be so bad after all.

"We didn't actually *catch* them," said William.

"We more or less did," retorted Tilly, spluttering a little, as her mouth was full of cream cake.

"We gave information that led to their arrest and charge," returned William. "But that was good enough."

"We're going to get the reward," said Tilly, her mouth empty now.

"Have you decided what to spend it on?" asked Mr Sheridan, who had come to join them.

"Well, *either* a holiday to Spain or a computer or a new bike and some clothes for me and my mum. There's loads of things that I'd like."

"Me too," agreed William.

"But what we think we might do," Tilly went on, "is go to Spain with my mum and William's mum. The four of us. His dad doesn't want to go. He says it would be too hot for him."

"Sounds like an excellent idea," said Mr Sheridan.

"You wouldn't like to come with us?"

He laughed. "I hardly think so. I'm a bit old for gadding about. No, you'll have to tell me all about it when you come back."

"It's amazing," said Cecil, "getting a reward of a thousand pounds!"

Tilly looked thoughtful. "I wonder if there could be any other badger-baiters in the area?"

"Tilly," said Mr Sheridan, his eyes twinkling, "I think maybe we've had enough excitement for a while!"

ORCHARD BOOKS

Orchard books are available from all good book shops,
or can be ordered direct from the publisher:
Orchard Books, PO BOX 29, Douglas IM99 1BQ
Credit card orders please telephone 01624 836000 or fax 01624 837033
or visit our Internet site: www.wattspub.co.uk
or e-mail: bookshop@enterprise.net for details.

To order please quote title, author and ISBN
and your full name and address.
Cheques and postal orders should be made payable to 'Bookpost plc.'
Postage and packing is FREE within the UK
(overseas customers should add £1.00 per book).

Prices and availability are subject to change.